Edward C. Billings

A Biographical Sketch of Emily Sanford Billings

Edward C. Billings

A Biographical Sketch of Emily Sanford Billings

ISBN/EAN: 9783743373013

Manufactured in Europe, USA, Canada, Australia, Japa

Cover: Foto ©Raphael Reischuk / pixelio.de

Manufactured and distributed by brebook publishing software
(www.brebook.com)

Edward C. Billings

A Biographical Sketch of Emily Sanford Billings

EMILY SANFORD BILLINGS

Faithfully yours
Emily S. Billings

DEDICATION

TO MY SWEET MOTHER,

HEPSEY DICKINSON BILLINGS,

I dedicate this Sketch, with the hope that, even by a tie so frail and perishable as words of mine, may be linked the memory of her, who first revealed to me the sacredness in woman's character, with that of her who, in all the relations of life, so conspicuously and endearingly illustrated that sanctity; that these two beings who had, as typical mother and wife, successively stood by my side, like angels, inciting to all that was good and repelling all that was bad, and who first met as seraphs in Heaven, might each occupy her own fitting relations to the worth herein recorded, the one having prepared me by the hints and suggestions from the depths of her own serene and loving nature, to regard as possible, and appreciate, when found, the more broadly unfolded and more brilliantly beautified excellencies of the other. Thus may there be a remembered association between her who foreshadowed and prefigured and her who also attained to and embodied in a shining life, such unworldliness, such affinity with goodness, such steadfastness for the right, and such purposes born of Heaven.

DEDICATION

PREFACE

This sketch was undertaken for several reasons.

Upon the death of the fondly loved, there abides for the survivor an everywhere-diffused, ever-present sense of loss, of the oppression of pain and solitude, a void co-extensive with mental associations,—almost an absence of what made existence personal.

Slowly, sometimes not till life on earth becomes nearly all a retrospect,—its chastening all wrought into character,—comes to the mourner from out the "ashes" of the grave the promised "beauty"—comes that ideal presence of our cherished dead which to the Spiritual Senses brings something of the look and fellowship, the high and brave encouragement, the restfulness, the assuagement, and the beckoning upward of their living selves.

"The prospect and horizon gone," every landscape is dreary, every shore barren. Our being, which yesterday was full of vigor and crowned with verdure, is to-day withered as if smitten by the killing frost; so that the utterly bereaved seems to be separated, far away, from

his own life. The connection between the soul and interest in external objects is paralyzed.

"As deep has thus called unto deep," "His waves and billows going over me," every phase and incident of the life herein outlined has won me to its contemplation, as, in some sense, to a communion with that vanished life. The labor of the sketch, therefore, has afforded some little relief amid the distraction of grief and the desolation of loneliness.

Also have I felt that the events of a life which had been one high, unbending resolve to be and to do what was pure and good and noble, wherein had been combined an intellect of such comprehensiveness, equipoise, and brilliancy with a disposition so sweet and joyous and loving and faithful, wherein had been reflected such love of justness and such generosity, and wherein acquirements had been gained with such sincerity and worn so unostentatiously,— a life that had engaged the interest and won the affection of so many gifted people,— should, along with her letters, so rich in thought, so elevated in sentiment, and so splendid in diction, with suitable grouping, have commemoration and permanence, which arrangement in a published volume could alone secure.

I knew, too, that her friends would find solace, and all would derive encouragement, in reading of the grace and sweetness with which she continued to invest life, as with a garment, under greatest trials, to the very last; of the heroism with which she encountered dangers, the resignation with which she endured pain, and the faith with which she triumphed in death.

Since a noble life transcends all other sources of human power for good, it has been my wish that, through faithful and appreciative narrative, the life of Emily Sanford may, with all its high consecration and pure affiliations, still flow on, a perpetual stream of beneficent influences — unceasingly reflecting tribute to the dead and incentive to the living.

As to the manner in which this purpose has been executed, provided only it shall have been accomplished and the record shall fittingly present the exquisite beauty and rare virtues of the life committed to it, I have a single ambition,— that it may in all respects be exactly such as her taste would approve. Not exactly will the asperity of criticism be softened, but rather the spirit of criticism will withdraw itself, where what has been written has been the spontaneous, well-nigh involuntary product of sorrow, born of a fullness of love between the subject and writer, which made them the whole world to each other, and makes what used to seem his worth towards her now to seem to need forgiveness.

EDWARD C. BILLINGS.

New Orleans, April 23d, 1886.

A BIOGRAPHICAL SKETCH

OF

.EMILY SANFORD BILLINGS

I

Early Life and Home Associations.

EMILY SANFORD was born on the 23d day of April, 1830. She was the youngest of eight children, five sons and three daughters. One of her brothers, Henry, who gave, perhaps, most brilliant promise of all this talented family, died when about to graduate in the Law School at Yale College. Another brother, Alfred, being possessed of an unconquerable passion for the sea, started on a sailing vessel for a voyage round the world. The vessel was never heard from. It was a fact, I have heard her state, that her mother, down to the time of her death, though so many years had elapsed since her son had gone forth, would start with a strange expectancy—like that feeling, half expectation, half despair, with which we still listen for the footsteps of those known to be dead—whenever she saw approaching her, on the street, any one clad in the garb of a sailor, hoping without any reason, and against reason, that she might discern in him traces of her handsome, unreturning boy. How long and how fervently hope of his reappearance was cherished by the family is beautifully evidenced by the will of her father, Hervey Sanford, who for nearly thirty years, and down to the year 1860, continued in his will and its codicils ample provisions for this long-absent son whom the sea never brought back.

Though I never personally knew her parents, I can readily describe her father. The clear features of his character are before my mind like the well-defined parts of an old line-engraving. He

was born of a family which, every Sabbath, from
end to end of that long dining-room in Bethany,
extended a bountifully supplied table, received
the whole body of worshipers, from far and
near, congregated for worship in the closely
adjoining church, and entertained them with
the simplicity and open-handed hospitality of
the old English barons. He had the great
merits of self-made men. What if he had some
of their faults? He was possibly severe in his
views of family government. Perhaps he sym-
pathized not enough with pastime and recrea-
tion. But his love for his family was intense,
sleepless, ever wise. He educated them in the
best seminaries in the land. He taught them
methods, the clearest and most precise, and
purposes which led to honor and distinction.
He acquired and bequeathed to them a fortune which has made his children and their children affluent; and along with this he handed
down to them a name that was a synonym
of integrity, and an example which, though it
lacked, possibly, sentimentality, was filled with
the heroic determination to subordinate wishes

to judgment and the indulgencies of to-day to provision for to-morrow.

I have difficulty in attempting a delineation of her mother. There has been such unanimity of so many voices attesting her high endowments as woman and mother; I entered so fully into the depth and tenderness of the feeling which dwelt in her who told me most of that mother; there was such a softening of the voice and often such suffusion of the eye accompanying her descriptions and allusions, that I have come to contemplate that mother as a character of such rounded fullness of rarest qualities that I fear lest I may fail to reproduce with completeness its exquisite symmetry and beauty.

She had a superior intellect, had been educated by an exalted mother; she was a good observer, was fond of books, was systematic in her ways of thought and life, was quick to perceive and keen to enjoy humor. The gentleness even of mothers was in her softened. Her endowments were all beautified by this, that the great law of her being was to love. Partly by inheritance, and partly by her own researches, while she presided with such dignity over her own house, she collected a system of ideas upon house-wifery that gave it the elegance and attractive-ness of one of the fine arts. Retaining in advanced age all her love of nature, when almost three-score and ten years old, she journeyed with as little weariness and as much amusement as do the young. At the age of seventy, sudden emo-tion caused the ruddy blush to mantle her cheek through her transparent skin, smooth as that of childhood, and all the delights of life brought to her unwearied heart, joy, in freshness like that of youth. She and this youngest daughter! How shall I find words to give, even in outline, the large affection that bound them together? The mother enveloped the daughter in a love that was like a shining atmosphere. The daughter, walking in its glad radiance, ren-dered back an homage of heart and life that was akin to a consecration.

There was another member of this family, the maternal grandmother, Mrs. Lyman, known in those days of plain, expressive names as

Polly Lyman, who was a person of such faculties and tastes that she naturally exercised a
controlling influence, even in a family so intellectual and refined as those who knew the
family of Hervey Sanford intimately felt it to
be. Her love of flowers, like her enthusiasm
in cultivating all that was high in aim and
pure in thought, was as vigorous in age as in
youth. Her wisdom embodied in many trite
sayings, her learning in the direction of Biography and History, her character (meaning by
that her decided qualities of heart and brain), are
handed down with admiration, not alone in Mr.
Sanford's family, but also among the children's
children of the circle in which she exerted so
great an influence.

I add a pen-and-ink picture of Mrs. Lyman
from an article published in 1870 in *The New
Haven Palladium*, entitled "Temple Street,
Forty Years Ago." The writer says:

"Mrs. Sanford's mother, Mrs. Lyman, lived
with them, and her specialty was a fondness
for flowers, which she cultivated herself in their
large garden with great success. I can see

her now, scissors in hand to cut flowers for a friend, stopping here and there to pull an interloping weed, or break off a dead leaf, her face lighting up to give pleasure, by a gift much rarer then than now. Her fondness for flowers and books was greatly in advance of her time.

"She was a great reader, and spent more money for books than, I'll venture to say, did many of her more carefully educated and younger neighbors. Books for mere reading were scarce and a luxury, and buying many was considered an extravagance."

In this family, at what then was known as 144 Temple street, where is most full the verdure and most striking the Gothic arch of the elms planted by Mr. Hillhouse, which have given to New Haven such an unchallenged name for shade and beauty, were passed the childhood and early youth of Emily Sanford. Here she learned to walk without first creeping. Here her infant lips uttered that first sentence, which she often gleefully recited, and which showed her characteristic independence, made up of so much sweetness, so much inflexibility, because of the wholeness, the unreservedness of her convictions. Here she commenced life with that fervent love for her mother which ever continued to be stimulus and restraint from girlhood, when, no matter how absorbing the visit or the sport, the sound of the clock, reminding her of her mother's injunction, always hurried her home, down to that long vigil, by day and by night, beside that dying mother's bed, when the passing away of the mother was followed by a swoon, like that of death, of the exhausted daughter.

Here she loved all her brothers and sisters with warm devotion. Here she loved her brother "Charlie," who was afterwards eminent at the New York bar, and one of the judges of the Superior Court of the City of New York. These two, the youngest of the family, drawn together in youth by a similarity of tastes and a unity of ideal in life, as man and woman taking their separate parts in the world, never lost the pure affection which had so beautifully characterized them as boy and girl. As a little boy, he suspended his ball-

playing the moment his little sister expressed
a wish to go home, gallantly escorted her to
and from school, and lovingly helped her over
the little pools of water left by the passing
showers. As a man, pressed by the cares and
labors of his exhaustive professional life, with
the same alacrity he interrupted his business
to welcome her or to accompany her wherever
her interests or wishes called her to go. Their
strikingly similar features were scarcely more
alike than were their characters. How was
her great love for him shown by the pride
and pleasure with which she lingered upon even
his name as she pronounced it! With what care
did she cherish before his death, and with what
reverence did she treasure afterwards, his boy-
ish birthday gift, his miniature painted on ivory,
set in a locket and resting on a tiny easel!
Well might she have clung to it with such
fond admiration! There was "such wondrous
purpose in his eyes" as they looked forth from
beneath that broad brow in that seraphic picture! This portrait, made when he was fourteen
years old, surpasses, in beauty of lineament as

3

it does in the evidence of lofty character, in spiritual expression, those pictures of the youthful Lord Byron which are regarded as types of beauty.

Generous, unforgetting brother, refined, unworldly man, who shrank from low and vulgar thoughts as from crimes; who climbed to a summit as an advocate and counselor, and who, though life was ended amidst prolonged sickness and at midday, crowned that life with a judicial fame even then resplendent! What wonder that such a sister grieved at the death of such a brother as though a part of her own life had expired.

Says a gifted woman who, like her, was born beneath the Temple street elms, and was the intimate friend of her mother and who knew the interior of the family well: "She was the pet of the household, but her sweet nature carried her through childhood and youth without inducing the selfishness or willfulness usually the result of such indulgence.

"She was an uncommon child, wide awake and playful, but with a directness and earnestness rarely seen so early in life.

" When a little girl, her mother sent her to her father's store for something for which she was in a hurry. The clerk proposed to send it. No, she would carry it. ' But,' said he, ' for a little lady to take such a package is not respectable.' ' Give it to me,' she exclaimed, 'and I will make it respectable,' and carried it off.

" Whatever she thought right and proper she would do, and no mere conventionality or adverse judgment could induce her to step out of the path which, according to her conviction, right and duty marked out for her."

II

At Mount Holyoke Seminary.

WHEN sixteen years of age she went to Mount Holyoke Seminary at South Hadley, Massachusetts.

During our married life I accompanied her upon the occasion of her revisiting that institution. Her account there and on the way, giving her hopes and efforts within those walls, which during her student life had been unadorned, but then inclosed much luxury, was full of brilliant anecdote and melting reminiscence, and disclosed the record of one who saw so exclusively the good, the beautiful, and the true, that it was like the lifting of the veil from the noblest of lives by a disembodied soul.

As showing the earnestness and elevation of her purposes during her school days, I insert extracts from a letter written by her in 1853 to her cousin, Ellen Hetzel, then a student at the seminary, for which I am indebted to the great kindness of Mrs. Frances L. (Kent) Knowlton, who was permitted to take a copy, who preserved it all these years, and who writes that "it had exercised a great formative influence upon her character, and, in her opinion, should be read to every class of young ladies at the seminary":

" Thank you for the introduction you have given me to your new friends. . . . Tell me what makes them your friends ; it is a sweet study — that of learning *what* makes other hearts congenial to our own. You fear you have disappointed Miss G. Do not stop to repent it, do not even stay to decide if the fact be really such, but *be* now what she *did expect* of you. It is never too late. Begin now to be too generous to see the faults of others, too noble to proclaim them. At school one only has to deserve approbation, and the winning it is sure.

" To command respect, one has but to master every lesson thoroughly, thus proving one's natural abilities; and to win love, one need only be worthy of it, as obliging, self-forgetting people ever are.

" The *noble* dignify employments be they ever so mean, but the insignificant must derive all their dignity from their employments. I respect myself so much when I have accomplished some task which others would shrink from as too far below them; and self-respect is more valuable than even renown, for it is never falsely won. It is easy to deceive others, but very difficult to deceive one's self."

Here she became much loved by that magnificently endowed woman, Mary Lyon. Here she formed a friendship for another teacher, hardly less talented, which blossomed like a perennial rose-tree throughout her life. Here she easily won the respect and attachment of classmates and fellow-pupils to which she and they ever clung with a tenacity rarely beheld. Between herself and one of these fellow-pupils the attachment then formed became and continued through life like that between sisters, beautifying the existence of each while she was in health, and hallowing by the tenderness of its mutual expression the moments among her latest on earth. Writing since her death, this fellow-pupil says: "In early life I gave to Emmie a large share of affection which grew with my growth and strengthened with my strength. Her appreciation of every loving word and thought made me, when I was not with her, look forward to her coming North with impatience."

There was a third friend whose childhood home had been so near to hers that from window to window they could almost join hands ; whose heart was ever as near to hers as had been home to home ; whose gentle voice and light step were ever music to her ear, and whose endeared presence had brought joy or comfort in thousands of life's varied experiences. These three friends ! what a beautiful picture did they make in her overflowing eyes, and afterwards, in her faithful memory, as they stood, gathered to utter their annual sweet farewell, grouped upon the door-step of the old Temple street house, with the autumn winds swaying and murmuring in the overhanging elms, playfully vieing with each other for her last salutation, and finally breathing their triple benediction as she drove away to commence her southward journey !

Another kindred spirit, an uninterruptedly and fondly lovèd and loving schoolmate at the seminary, one of whose letters, written from Dresden, contained the last written words of affection received by her on earth, writes since her death : " There is no one outside my immediate family whose death could have so overcome me as does Emily's. The world seems darker and

poorer for her loss, and I can look forward joyfully to the time when I, too, may lay my burden
down and go to her in some of the many man-
sions prepared for the ransomed ones."

Here at the seminary, too, she felt the influence of divine grace, and enjoyed vivid religious
experiences. The severe winters in that latitude
told upon her physical organization and caused
an illness which somewhat interrupted her progress in her studies; but she left the seminary,
carrying with her acquisitions in her knowledge
which her quick perception, energy, and industry
rendered unusually extended, with the stimulus
and suggestions which contact with such an order
of minds as were teachers in that school of learning must give, and with her affections enriched
by friendships, the delightful intimacies of which
death alone interrupted.

III

Travel Abroad.

IN 1851 she went abroad with her sister Catharine, Mrs. Bliss, and her brother-in-law, George Bliss. The circumstance of her going and being with Mr. and Mrs. Bliss while she was in Great Britain, aided her much in the harvest of ideas which she gathered abroad. For they at that time lived in England, and thus she saw, through them and their friends, English life and English homes; and, too, they were of such active minds and discriminating judgments as to aid vastly a younger traveler capacitated and eager to learn.

But her observations upon the Continent, as well as in England, must have been of a thoughtful and thorough character, for she had derived such rare and complete knowledge as enabled her to give, in after years, not alone an account of meritorious works of art and memorable beauties of scenery, but to combine and blend all with

4

great events of history, and, what is far more unusual and a far better test of talent in the voyager, to give you in a word an estimate of the various peoples and to explain their national and local traits.   Of all those who have sojourned abroad, from whom I have been privileged to derive ideas freely through daily conversation, I think her conceptions and inferences were the most vividly clear, most thoroughly founded, and most valuable in their application to daily living.

As showing the child-likeness of her nature and her deep love for friends at home, I make an extract from a letter written by her, when in Paris, to the teacher-friend whom she had so learned to love and who had so learned to love her at the Mount Holyoke Seminary.   She writes: "I would gladly relinquish all this for one quiet hour with you.   It would be no sacrifice to me, love, to exchange the allurements of this beguiling metropolis for your quiet home."

I insert extracts from one of her published letters written from London upon

THE TOWER, THE ABBEY, THE PALACES, AND
HYDE PARK, IN LONDON.

IV

Her Letters.

THE ABBEY AND THE TOWER.

"BUT St. Paul's had little interest for me compared with that which Westminster Abbey inspired. If you would learn life's meaning or death's reality; if you would know the emptiness of fashion, gold, and fame, or realize the worth of time, you should visit Westminster Abbey, where the head that schemed and toiled for power, the form before which nations bowed, the heart that bled for fame, and the tawdry leader of a butterfly chase, lie paralyzed in death.

"The world seems but a petty stage when one looks upon its famous actors stripped of their theatrical accoutrements, and, wearied with the toil of their exciting parts, sleeping the same untroubled sleep — the tyrant and the victim — power and weakness — riches and poverty — side by side.

"How empty seem life's glittering baubles when one sees the robe of state replaced by the winding-sheet; how vain its wide distinctions when the mightiest monarch, like his humblest subject, yields to the same King, Death; how childish seem the heart's strongest passions, when one thinks of the vast multitude who loved and hated — gloried and despaired — sorrowed and rejoiced — who suffered and enjoyed, centuries ago, as we are doing now! Ambition's frenzied dream, the mind's electric flashes, love's delirious happiness, will soon be to us what they have long been to them.

"I have heard many a sermon from the text, 'Vanity of Vanities, *all is vanity*,' but it was not until I trod these antique aisles that its reality came over me with all the force of actual truth, and sent me forth into the world again with a wiser but a sadder heart."

THE TOWER.

"You know that at school my favorite study was history; but I never read such thrilling pages of it in any book as one finds written all over the walls of yonder old gray tower.   You ask me to tell you of Castles, Palaces, and Monuments ; and *there* all the three are comprised in one ; for surely no monument could be more teeming with records of the past than this very tower — so famous as the palace, the fortress, and the prison of by-gone years. It is interesting to the artist for its picturesque situation on the banks of the Thames ; to the anti-quary, as a relic of William the Conqueror's time ; and, more than all, to the historian, as the scene of those national dramas whose influence on the country and its people is even now discernible.

"The *stone stairs*, beneath which were buried the bodies of the infant princes, were all I saw of Richard's bloody tragedy ; and the heading-block and axe that formed the closing scene of Essex's life are now the only traces left of the comedy of vanity performed by the ruffled queen who played her cards so well, till *hearts* were trumps.   One *hears* of things like these with that kind of interest we give to romance spun from fancy's web ; but it is with a different feeling than one looks upon the very field where the battle of life was fought.

" I have seemed to read a *living* history since the day I sat in Sir Walter Raleigh's dungeon, and trod the prison floor of Anne Boleyn, Mary Stuart, and the Lady Jane Grey. The faded relics of former grandeur tell their stories of the quondam palace ; the moat around the buildings marks the fortress ; and the warders, dressed in the costume they wore in the Elizabethan age, remind the visitor of the old tower's prison days.

" Every stranger is led through sundry long, dark, narrow passages into a tiny closet, occupied by a wizened crone, the impersonation of one's fancy picture of the Witch of Endor. She is habited in a blue petticoat and a stiffly starched short gown, and hanging from her waist is the ponderous key to the iron-bound door that opens upon the regalia.   Here, one is forcibly reminded of the old aphorism about 'riches taking to themselves wings,' by the *iron cage* which incloses the royal paraphernalia, and by the *heavy chains* that attach each article to its place.   Thereby hangs an omen of the connection between the palace and the prison.   The jargon of the old woman, who strove to teach us that those four walls comprised 'all the kingdoms of the world, and she their sovereign was,' wearied me; and the gold and jewels seemed of far less worth than the *lives* that had been pawned for them. So I quickly turned away from the Crown beneath which so many heads had ached, and the scepter that bloody hands had swayed, to breathe a *freer* air; for the atmosphere of those prison walls oppressed my heart with the great truths that since the morning had been sealed thereon. But I shall spend another day at the Tower before we leave London, for well I know that it teaches lessons more wise, truths more profound, than all the books man's pen ever wrote."

THE PALACES OF LONDON.

"The present palaces of London rather disappoint my expectations as to *outward* grandeur, but, *within*, nothing can exceed their luxurious elegance. Kensington Palace, where the childhood of Queen Victoria was spent, is extremely irregular in structure; and St. James's, where she still holds her levees, *appears* more like a huge pile of bricks than a royal dwelling-place; but within its portals there are saloons of immense size, magnificently decorated. Buckingham Palace forms the winter home of the Royal Family; but even *that* would be quite unpretending, if it were not for the charm of a situation in Hyde Park. It has little merit in an architectural point of view, for it is only a combination of many different designs that from time to time have remodeled and enlarged without improving its appearance, and left at last the Buckingham House of George the Third's reign, modernized."

HYDE PARK.

" Far away to the westward of the vast and crowded metropolis, stretches the three hundred and fifty acres of open ground known as Hyde Park, beautifully diversified with grassy hillocks, clover-grown knolls, and tiny moss-lined valleys. Through it flow the clear waters of the Serpentine, reflecting flowery banks and the leafy branches of tall trees that rock the nests of summer birds whose thrilling melodies the very beggars are rich enough to buy.

"I never saw anything half so perfect as this lovely picture of the country, spread out in the very heart of a great city, to refresh with equal benefit careworn inhabitants of narrow, thickly crowded alleys, and the sicklier cheeks of the *more* crowded drawing-room occupants. It gives a charming feature to a city landscape, especially in the eye of one who comes from a land where the feverish eagerness to turn everything into gold is always drowning the voice of Nature in the noisy din of business — where trees are only beautiful for the cords of wood they will make, and pleasure grounds are eye-sores because they '*might* have been sold for three hundred pence,' and turned to mechanical uses !

"You should see Hyde Park of a Sunday, to get an idea of London's population and London's wealth. You would think it were some gala day, as your eye wandered over the motley throng of showily dressed people who are then sure to fill this favorite resort. It seems like a triumphal procession — the long line of stylish-looking equipages that extends from one end to the other of those immense grounds. There are majestic

5

cavaliers beside splendid carriages filled with beautiful women in costly robes — decorated with golden crests, and drawn by superb horses guided by coachmen in powdered wigs and gay liveries.   The footpaths, too, are thronged with people from a humbler walk of life — people in their holiday dresses and their holiday smiles! The effect is so imposing, that if you were to see only the kaleidoscope views of life that one gets in Hyde Park of a Sunday afternoon, you would take it for an Elysium of beauty and pleasure, rather than the thing of toil and care and sorrow that it is.   But the every-day side of the picture would quickly break the spell.   All the live-long week, misery and want and wretchedness are toiling in the self-same thoroughfares, with aching limbs and breaking hearts and tearful eyes; for one-half the world *must* toil and sweat and groan, that the other half may thrive and rejoice.   The London streets are thronged with hoary heads tottering to the grave and craving charity to pay their way, and with tiny feet just pattering into life, that are already learning to keep time to the beggar's voice.   I wonder if I shall ever get hardened to the piteous tales that startle one's ears at every step, and the ragged types of suffering that make one's eyes wet and one's heart sick."

After her return from Europe, cultured as she was by her studies at the schools, by much travel and by social intercourse with highly educated people, she seems to have loved to write.

I insert an extract from one of her published letters, written in 1855, on the "Mission of Woman," another from the same letter telling of the zest with which she had enjoyed a summer in "The West," and another extract from some published thoughts of hers on "The Closing Year."

WOMAN'S MISSION.

"To raise the fallen ; to relieve the oppressed ; to comfort the sorrowing ; to watch over the sick ; to be strength to the weary, help to the infirm, and light to the blind — this is woman's sphere ; and if her influence ever extend to political affairs, it is an influence as unseen as that with which Spring carpets the fields and freshens the trees —

such an influence as flowers have on poetry, as air has on music, as light has on life."

A HAPPY SUMMER IN THE WEST.

"But I am wandering from the luxuriance of life to its desolation. I began to tell you how much more beautiful has been this summer than any other summer I ever knew. Perhaps the change of climate has strengthened my nerves and brightened my vision; or, perhaps, being nearer sundown gives everything a softer radiance; at all events, I certainly do see things in a better light. I have looked at life through the laughing eyes of childhood and through the clearer eyes of youth, but it never before looked such a glad, bright, glorious thing. I have drank it from mountain rills and from city fountains, but it never seemed a luxury till now.

"There has been always a tone of sadness in my song that told of a cold and hollow, a blighting, bitter world; but of late the tune has changed. 'Oh World, with all thy faults I love thee still!'

"In other years I could have died unmurmur

ingly ; now, earth seems to obeautiful to leave, and every day I pray, 'oh let me live.' This season has been to me a volume of beautiful pictures, and upon each successively I have gazed with ever-new delight. I shall see the last leaf of Western scenery turn with inexpressible regret."

THE CLOSING YEAR.

"I remember to have seen in one of the watch factories in Geneva, Switzerland, a little statue of an auctioneer standing under a red flag, holding in his hand a time-piece. The man's attitude was so perfect, his expression so eager, so hurried and so alert, in short, the whole representation was so complete, that one's imagination endued the clock with a voice that made every tick seem to utter the word 'going.' It was a very pretty way of reminding everybody that time is going, going, going, that time may soon be gone. Longfellow attributes to the clock's voice the words 'for-ever — never.' Pierpont refers to the swinging pendulum as always whispering 'passing away,' and some other poet calls the clock's tick 'that voice which forbids procrastination by incessantly calling now, now, now.' To persons whose powerful imagination or acute sense of hearing thus invests matter with life, no better warning is needed, for such can see the sands of life wasting in an hour-glass, and the lamp of life go out in every sunset; such can hear requiems in the night wind, and read elegies in the fading leaves. But for the mass of men, whose thoughts are drowned in the noisy din of business, or whose perceptions are blunted by contact with the world, the anniversary holidays of Christmas and New Year are untold blessings. They are the observatories of life, whence men gaze out into the past and learn how much can happen in a year. From such a view, men come down better, if not happier. To mark attentively what *has* been, makes one tremble for what is to be. The light in the eye may fade, the rose on the cheek may pale, the light of the heart may imperceptibly lessen in the present, but in the pictures of the past these things strike us most startlingly."

I add an extract from a published letter upon

A REVISIT TO NIAGARA.

"Years ago, I had stood on the self-same spot and seen its flight as hurried, and its rapids dash and foam as wildly. Had they never rested since? Would they always keep pace with the flight of time? It tired me to think of it; so I turned away in search of the high rocks over which geography used to say 670,000 tons of water fall every moment. The mighty rushing sound of many waters proclaimed them near; and surrounding space echoed and reëchoed the words, 'Almighty, Eternal, Immutable,' from that voice of thunder which God tuned at the foundation of the world to sing His Omnipotence so long as time should last. The whole scene was as if I had left it only yesterday; the river still flowed on over its emerald bed, and the foaming cataract was sending up its incense of spray, now as before.

"Fowler, the famous phrenologist, once told me that I had no bump of *Reverence*, and others vainly have tried to excite the emotion since.

" The idols to which Society bows have always seemed, like myself, of the earth, earthy, and I have scorned to yield homage to such; but Niagara, the unfathomable, all-conquering and resistless, the magnificently terrible and overwhelmingly grand, seemed a fit shrine at which to bend, and involuntarily I knelt before it, under the influence of a strange awe that would have trembled into actual fear, had I not chanced to raise my eyes and see God's bow of promise lying on the Lunar Fall.' Then I remembered, that though Niagara was great, He that created Niagara is greater.

" The crushed violets beneath me sent forth perfume to whisper that their tiny lives were nourished by the cataract's spray; and little birds sang sweetly over their torrent home, knowing that 'He careth for them.' So I said to myself, 'Are you not of more value than many sparrows?' and went on my way along the precipice's edge, and, like the flowers and the birds, was not afraid."

Her description of her loved New Haven and of the bells summoning to church on the Sabbath morning there, will, by its fidelity and vividness, bring the place and hour before all familiar with them :

" The surrounding hills, which by right belong to the Green Mountains of Vermont, look down upon an unbroken level that is divided into squares by streets lined with magnificent elms, so placed at regular intervals that the interlaced branches of opposite trees form, from one extremity of a street to another, the most perfect arch. These trees, gigantic in size and most luxuriant in foliage, are said to have resulted from a poet's dream of beauty, and to have been planted some seventy years ago by a poet's hand. Be that as it may, they have christened their dwelling-place with a most poetical sobriquet, *'The City of Elms.'*

" *'City of Steeples'* would be an appropriate. name, for I never saw so many churches within so small a compass. As you sit at the Tontine of a Sunday morning, and hear the holy Sabbath stillness broken by the loud, clear music of their various bells, each within a stone's-throw of the other, and all blending in the most perfect harmony, you seem to have found your way nearer to Heaven

6

than you ever were before.   Then, when the last
throng you have watched crossing the neatly kept
green disappears from your sight, and the church
doors close, leaving the great outer temple de-
serted, involuntarily you wander forth, wooed by
the cool, inviting shade, and entranced by the
music of the myriads of birds that build in the old
elm boughs without any one to molest or make
them afraid.   You would find it no difficult matter
to imagine yourself in the Garden of Eden, and
easily forget that man was driven forth to earn
his bread by the sweat of his brow.

"The society of New Haven must be highly
intelligent and refined, for the venerable seat of
learning in their midst makes the interest of the
people collegiate rather than commercial, and
gives a literary tone to everything in its vicinity."

I add her account of an orphan whom she saw
in the Asylum there, and of her deep and intense
feelings in contemplating one so young, so beautiful, and so unfortunate:

"A striking instance of this unequal distribu-
tion of fortune's favors came within my sphere of
observation in New Haven.   At the Orphan

Asylum of that place I saw twenty-five or thirty children of various ages, between three and twelve. There were bright-eyed boys and laughing-lipped girls sitting in their little school-room when I entered. They were singing ' I want to be an angel,' and most of them looked to be so much of the earth, earthy, that I couldn't help thinking through what a long series of transmigrations their souls would have to pass before they could realize their wish to change the human into divine.

" But, amid the crowd of little faces uplifted to watch the visitors whose idle curiosity they were trained to satisfy, I really saw but one. A little girl, of infantile proportions and baby features, threw over me a spell which it was impossible to arrest or displace. I cannot tell you whether she was a blonde or brunette. I did not even guess her age or learn her name, but I am sure she will haunt me forever. She carried about her some strange charm that with magnetic power drew her to my heart, and left there the picture of a cherub that comes up before me to illustrate the pen of every poet, and to rival the dream of every artist. I found her, as it were, something I had wanted all my life-long without knowing it, and there she stood, just within my reach and yet so far beyond it.

"To me there is something heart-rending in the sight of a motherless child. Like some lone bark, tossed by mighty billows, I tremble for it. My heart yearns for it, and my hand involuntarily stretches out to protect it. I want to shelter it in my own arms, cradle it on my own breast, comfort it all my life; and yet, as I sat there among those poor little orphans, with the tears rolling down my cheek, I seemed to forget them all in one, or rather to concentrate the misery of all in that one whom I longed to secure from sorrow and misfortune. I drew the little creature to my side, caught her in my arms, and kissed her time and time again. She received my caresses in the most matter-of-course way, and heard my praises as heedlessly as if she had been used to them all her life. Other children gathered around, envyingly, and seemed to crave the notice which she so lightly esteemed; and if it had been money they asked, I could have easily scattered it among them, but my affections went forth only to her.

" This is only a single instance ; but the ' New Testament' will give you another ; for, though it mentions many men who came to our Saviour, of only *one* does it say, ' Now, when Jesus looked upon the young man, He loved him.' "

V

Interest in Lady Franklin.

BUT of all her published thoughts, those which attracted most attention and elicited most admiration, not only from scholars, but also from all generous-minded people, were her soul-stirring appeals, written and published with a view to arouse public and individual efforts for the discovery of the *fate which had overtaken Sir John Franklin.* I subjoin an extract from one of these fervent letters :

" ' Hope deferred maketh the heart sick.' Go, ask the Lady Franklin what that saying meaneth. She has watched for steps that come not ; she has long and vainly listened for a once familiar voice. She has seen the fairest hopes a fond heart ever cherished grow ripe with expectation, only to fade and droop and die under the chilling blasts of disappointment.

" Day by day she has waited, trusted, believed, only to find patience, trust, and hope empty delusions, bitter mockeries, until days have grown into weeks, and months become years.

" Full well she knows the agony of harrowing suspense that fears to hope the best, and refuses to believe the worst; that clings to straws and chases fire-flies, pining for hope and yearning for light.

" Her busy thoughts have drawn from the long fibres of possibility every conceivable excuse for such unreasonable delay. Daylight fancies and nightly dreams have portrayed every variety of suffering to aggravate the already painful circumstances; for, while *the certainty* of evil has a *limit*, where the sufferer finds at least a resting-place, *suspense* is boundless, illimitable, reflecting itself in *everything*, until its cause is magnified a hundred-fold. Positive grief falls on the heart a heavy blow; but its hopelessness is its own cure. Time heals the wound and wears away the scar, and useless lamentation gives place to stoical indifference or heavenly resignation; but, in suspense, expectancy keeps the sorrow always fresh, the heart always sore, and the days and weeks and years that pass over it only serve to irritate and inflame the wound.

" Suspense is the slowest but surest canker that ever preyed upon human vitals; and there is no greater benefactor to his kind than he who endeavors to draw it from the heart doomed to its harrowing caprices. The generous and humane who have spent their energies or their wealth in search of certainty, by which to minister to minds long diseased with suspense, require no eulogies. In their *consciousness of magnanimity* have they their own exceeding great reward.

" The volunteers, who 'took their lives in their hands' and went forth over the pathless waves in search of the lost ones, needed not shouts of applause to mark their going, or triumphal processions to greet their return. Far across the sea, there dwells a noble heart whose thoughts and hopes followed them on all their dangerous way.

And 'He who keepeth the waters in the hollow of His hand,' listening to that lone heart's prayer for them, calmed the troubled waves and tempered the mighty winds, that they wafted the mariners safely home. And, though their trusty ships brought not the long-watched-for wanderer back again, the widowed one hailed joyfully their coming, even as she felt gratefully their going. The hopes and thanks and prayers of such a soul, are they not pearls of great price? I have no words in which to express my admiration of the noble Lady Franklin. She is an honor to my sex, such as the records of time have known of but few.

"The fortitude, energy, and perseverance which have characterized her during all the season of trial, which would have entirely paralyzed most women, must win for her the respect of all mankind, even as it has enlisted the earnest sympathies of the whole civilized world. A sincere Christian, a model wife,

"'A perfect woman, nobly planned.'

"Such, I am sure, is the Lady Jane — fit helpmeet for such a husband as the noble patriot, the brave seaman, the generous, self-sacrificing Sir John Franklin.

"The world is ringing with this earnest cry — '*Wanted*—Hearts to feel for the sufferings of the perishing—hands to relieve the necessities of the destitute—and minds to determine for them the simplest and surest mode of relief.'

"If so deep the interest felt for those who attempt to settle this doubtful question, what words can paint the warm glow of sympathy that will kindle in every heart when this crisis of suspense is passed, and the world breathes forth its welcome to the wanderer, its blessing on his saviour? For whom is reserved that honorable title? The Roman triumphs were not so great, for they rejoiced over the lost; here will be the holy gratitude of the saved. The Grecian conquests were not so bold, for they did not overcome unknown obstacles."

Henry Grinnell, whose philanthropy in furnishing vessels for the Arctic Expedition is remembered with patriotic pride by every American, so forcibly felt the magnanimity and power of those letters, that he gave a dinner in honor of

7

their author. The entertainment was given on Bond street, in the city of New York, in the year 1854. A distinguished company was present to meet her, among them Dr. Elisha Kent Kane, who published "A Narrative of the Expedition in search of Sir John Franklin."

She received, also, from Lady Franklin herself, a letter in which she expressed her deep sense of gratitude for those valued appeals to the American mind in behalf of herself and her knowledge-loving husband.

The letters from which the foregoing extracts have been made are characterized by such precision in idea and expression, by such comprehensiveness and condensed and sustained energy of thought, by such beauty and grandeur of imagery, and by such elevation and tenderness of feeling; the fire and touch of genius is so unmistakably in them, and to such a degree had she interested intellectual people in her writings, that success and fame of no mean order were already assured to her in the walks of literature, had she continued in them.

VI

Life as the Wife of Captain James F. Armstrong.

IN January, 1858, she intermarried with Captain James F. Armstrong, of the United States Navy. He was a gentleman of excellent family, was a member of the Society of the Cincinnati, was a man of unusual intelligence, great frankness of character, polished manners, and abounded in agreeable information which he had gathered in his intercourse with a large circle of highly educated friends, and in the multiplied and varied voyages he had made as naval commander.

His was a tender and affectionate nature towards which children were always drawn. He was not only a husband, ever kind and devoted, but he was a lover throughout his married life. I knew him through others, chiefly through her, and it was impossible not to feel admiration for his character. " Good, kind, true, noble-hearted, high-minded man": these are the words with which I find she characterized him in her diary upon one of the recent anniversaries of his death, and his whole life showed that they were richly deserved.

As his wife, her social life was largely with those brilliant men who then constituted our naval commanders, and their not less brilliant wives, at the various naval stations where her husband, Captain Armstrong, was in command. In these circles, the richness of her ideas, the sparkle of her conversation, and the generosity and gracefulness of her hospitality made her a shining ornament.

Their home life was that of two pure, confiding natures, striving tenderly to make each other happy, and with rare capacity to afford happiness. It was a union to which she brought the large purposes with which she ever enfolded those she loved. It was a union productive of mutual happiness, earnest and deep. It was severed by the death of Captain Armstrong, in the early part of the year 1873.

VII

Life as Wife of the Author.

ON the 20th day of October, 1874, we were married. The ceremony was performed by President Porter, who, in addition to his own relations as a friend to us, was the husband of that choice spirit who had been her mother's, and ever was her, true friend. He had been my professor when I was a student in Yale College. We were married in New Haven, in Centre Church, where, for the period of fifty-eight years, her parents had worshiped, the calm air and sacred associations of which she had enjoyed throughout childhood and youth, and almost on the very spot, where, twenty years before, I had stood in delivering my philosophical oration at Commencement.

O ye joys which beam upon and beckon to us from out the glad future which lies before all-expectant youth, and which ofttimes fade from us, obscured by the sorrows and narrowing struggles of later years, how did ye then come thronging back to me with your old-time, glowing aspect and with all the rapture and twice the tenderness of your early promise!

From the time when, in assuming our marriage vows, she placed her hand in mine, down to the hours when, cold and stiffening in death, I still clasped it, the grasp was as of a hand reached down from heaven, leading me thither. Our married life was to me "another morn risen on mid-noon." It was a long polar day, it was a "walk through meadows blossom-paved." She was so constituted as to gather the elements of content and diversion and progress from the small, as well as the great, events of life, and she poured forth her ever-renewed, exhaustless treasures of thought before her companion, keeping full every receptivity of enjoyment by her playfulness, her sympathies, her taste, and her culture.

Self-denying, self-forgetting, alike in sickness and in health, she followed me with unslumbering care and upward-tending suggestion like that of the ministering spirits sent forth from God.

Our enjoyment had the mellowness of the mid-day of life, along with the unabated freshness of its youth. It was found, not in idyllic leisure, but amid constant occupation, and would have been as complete and soul-satisfying without a luxury and in the straitened ways of poverty, or even by the road-side, as it was in our houses crowded with comforts. For it was above and beyond these accidents.

The radiant and pure spirit of beauty that walks hand in hand with true marriage, comes it like the wind which bloweth where it listeth, without visible origin? So that it is found, or, alas! missed without cause? O no; it emanates from what are among the most real, as well as the best, of human attributes. It has its origin and sustenance in mutual, implicit trust, "heart answering to heart as face to face in water"; in aims and aspirations formed and kept so plastic, so impressible, that similitude, almost identity, results; one string responding to another with music when it is not smitten, because the key or pitch is the same, and because there are borne to it by the pulses of the air its own cognate vibrations, awakening its note and compelling its response by that law of harmony which slumbers in all created things; in disinterestedness —in habitually, systematically finding truest development, highest satisfaction, by each in honor, in ease, and in happiness preferring the other.

In that awfully solemn and sublime Apocalypse, revealed in the Isle of Patmos to that "beloved disciple" who styles himself as " brother and companion in tribulation," the mystical suggestion of both David and Isaiah is adopted as a distinct symbol, and the Saviour and His organized followers are represented as " The Lamb " and " His Bride." The exalted possibilities, inhering in true marriage, it is, which caused it thus to stand forth as the divinely selected emblem of the ineffably holy intimacy and union between the Redeemer and His Church and make it forever true that, as in our Christian, so in our wedded life, may we "climb on stepping-stones of our dead selves to higher things."

Among those who shared with us our joy on the occasion of our marriage were an officer in our navy and his gentle and loving wife, whose joint friendship for us had such genial warmth and inventive constancy that from year to year it quickened our lives, like the sun's rays; and whose unostentatious, unslumbering, tender mutual devotion gave to their daily married life the rhythm and inspiration of a sweet, rich poem. These friends, journeying for years abroad, had obtained for us an oil-painting, the presentation of which had been unavoidably delayed until both fondly loved wives had gone from us, leaving earthly life naught but a picture, when one surviving husband in solitude delivered and the other in solitude received this now inexpressibly sacred token. The painting was of Iris, who in the early dawn, the earth still covered by the twilight beneath, is bearing in her pitcher, from the lakes and rivers to the clouds which are lighted up by the breaking day, the water which the poets fabled was to be returned to its sources in showers and dews. The mythological conception typifies with every auxiliary from art the ceaseless movement of the courses of nature; but the circumstances attending the execution of the gift proclaim, even from the grave to the grave, how incapable of stay or hindrance is the

8

current of human kindness, and how surely our affections and our purposes survive even our lives below.

We passed our winters in New Orleans, and
our summers in New Haven, proceeding from one
place to the other by easy journeys, and stopping
for rest for two or three days, either in Cincinnati
or Washington, according to the route which we
took.   The migrations were full of quiet advent-
ure which interested her attentive faculties, and in
themselves were scarcely more tiresome than the
annual flight and return of the birds. She reveled
in the bloom of the flowers and the unchecked verdure of the trees and plants in our Southern home,
in its clear mellow skies, in the airiness of character and manner which is found, not only in the
French-speaking portion of the citizens of New
Orleans, but to some extent among all, in the
amusements which are well-nigh perpetual, in the
hospitalities extended to famous people from
abroad, and in her elegant intercourse, in which
her amiable, warm-hearted nature delighted, with
those true and tried New Orleans friends whose
admiration for her was shown by the most thoughtful, unremitting kindness.

With equal zest and tenderer emotions did she come to the shade and coolness, the substantial thoughts, the delightfully intellectual atmosphere, to the friends of the heart, many and cultivated, to the drives by the indented and picturesque northern shore of the Sound and out upon the fragrant hills, to the leisure and rest and miscellaneous reading, to the old-time Sabbath worship, and to the loved guests — that filled the bright hours throughout the summer days of our Northern sojournings.

Without effort and unconsciously, in all this varied existence, she "decorated and cheered every sphere in which she moved, glittering like the morning star, full of life and joy and splendor."

Who that participated in conversation with her did not suspend it with regret and resume it with delight? finding therein fullness without satiety, variety without repetition or diffuseness, the utterance and perception of the nicest shades of humor, brilliancy which inflicted nor wound nor sting, all impelled and guided by a spirit as unflagging as that of the most moving orators.

This purpose, this habit of mind, it was that made her judgment on all subjects so well-nigh unfailing, that made her so painstaking in her inquiry, and so careful to expunge from the equation mere feeling. This, too, was the secret of her patience in hearing those who differed from her, and of her independence in her estimate of persons and events when finally reached; for the censure or approbation of others was valuable to her only as it had solid foundation.

She had within herself such resources for self-occupation and the entertainment of others, that the days when we were separated from the world by travel, or rain, or sickness were really the brightest.

Often when I would express some disquiet on leaving her in the morning for my court duties, lest she might not have enough to amuse her for the day, would she reply with a smile: "I have myself, my thoughts, my books, and my pen; I shall be entertained." It was not merely that she had abounding information, nor merely that she had it in her mind arranged in so orderly a manner as to be readily brought forward, nor merely that she had such quick sympathies and so constant a desire to make the time pass pleasantly as to make her explore with quickness and vigor the recesses of her mind for material for thought and intercourse, but it was the operation of all these advantages, together with a spirit of serene contentment such as the fabled wise were represented to have had, which was contagious, that made our days of isolation from our fellows seem all too few and too short.

Connected with this trait was her deep satisfaction with her own, which she cherished, not with the narrow purpose with which the miser hoards, but from that spirit which led her to invest with sacredness and dignity her personal existence and all that radiated from it. Never was a sweet thought or grateful association, once connected with an object, allowed in her mind to be dissevered from it. When her well-poised judgment had selected an article, or a friend, she rarely abandoned her choice. So far from the old and tried becoming in her eyes, from the lapse of time, wearisome,—fit to be supplanted by the new,— the passing years did but impart confirmation and

veneration to her preferences. Her memory was like a land abounding in altars which had been erected to, and were guarded for, those who had made her happy.

Her appreciation of kindness was new every morning and fresh every evening; was so natural, ingenuous, and varied, so from a child-like heart, that one forgot the possibility of weariness from any contributory effort, in the pleasure of witnessing her responsive delight in its reception.

How shall I express in fit words the fidelity of her nature — her unswerving adherence to a character or an act which she knew to deserve approbation? She admired and loved cautiously, and with keenest discrimination, but, when once her heart had been carried, nothing but discovered falsity could diminish her esteem or chill her affection. How cheerfully she endured, or rather how she gloried in, sacrifice for whom she loved! How bravely she stood up for the absent or the dead whom she had known favorably from history or in life, if their motives were called in question! In her deep nature, love and admiration seemed to be spontaneous, emotional, and enthusiastic, but seemed at the same time to have the uniformity, the fixedness, the unfailing certainty that belong to principles and convictions. With her, misfortune heightened excellence, and inability, on the part of the worthy, to repay kindness, moved her to redouble it. Her generosity was princely. In the selection of her objects of sympathy she so infallibly sifted the chaff from the wheat, her charity was measured by such judgment, and was administered with such infinite tact and such total absence of ostentation, that the world knew little of it. Her whole nature delighted in a generous act, and shrank from, and almost scorned, any outside echo from it, as if the renown from unselfish conduct marred its beauty. Her gifts were secret, unobserved of men, save by their recipients, falling "mutely, like the dew upon the hills." But they were incessant, inducing, of course, provision through more or less self-denial or the regulation of expenditures, and rendered doubly useful by her wise and timely bestowal. Whether, in obedience to the dictates of her sense of duty, and in spite of the remonstrances of almost all her friends, by a single conveyance she irrevocably granted well-

9

nigh half of her individual estate; or whether, with
almost filial love, she for years clothed some once
affluent, always and universally respected lady
whom poverty and affliction had flung far from
her elevated place in society, and reduced to
almost want, sharing her sorrows, supplying her
every need with such alacrity and enjoyment that
the blessing of the giver was, by both, felt to be
even greater than that of the receiver; whatever
she day by day did, in her original, beneficent
way of doing for others, was done not from a rap-
idly expended impulse to please by a donation,
but from the deep-rooted purpose to do good, to
do a loving and kind act, to heal some wound, to
assuage some sorrow. It was literal magnanimity,
the expansion, the reaching forth of a great soul
towards others, because it was its nature to act in
a manner truly great.

The readiness with which she entered into all
the favorable circumstances of life in New Orleans, the delightful constancy with which she
dwelt upon them, as well as the power with which
she could depict them, is strikingly shown in a
letter to a very dear friend, dated there in 1880,

She says : " I have tried St. Augustine, Jackson-
ville, and the other Florida resorts, and abominate
them all. They narrow life down to the very
necessities of existence, and it seems to me that
an invalid requires to be tempted with the luxuries
of life, and to be diverted from thoughts of pain
and despondency by the sight of, if not the par-
ticipation in, amusements. In New Orleans it is
possible to command every luxury which every
climate yields, and impossible to avoid amusement
if one took no trouble to procure it. Then, there
is so much beauty in the floral surroundings, and
so much to be learned of the peculiarities of the
people from their out-of-door life, that one cannot
fail to be entertained. There is so much of the
French element here that the streets are always
gay, and the predominance of the Catholic religion
gives one always one festival or another to cele-
brate."

What a shrine to her, what a repository of associations in which were blended a child's sus-
ceptibility and woman's deepest feelings, was the
old home in New Haven, where she was born and
where her youth was nurtured, where her parents

had lived half a century, and from which the dead of her family, whom she so loved, had been borne, appears in a letter to the same dear friend.   She says: "It hardly seems possible that in little more than a month I shall again see the dear old home and the familiar faces, but when I think of it my heart bounds.   Whenever I am sick elsewhere, it seems to me that if I were within those sacred walls within which I was born, and under those grand old elms, I should find an electric light that would have some healing power, and that even, if still suffering, I should in spirit be watched over and soothed by those who used to nurse me back to health in those delightful, long-ago years."

"With what measure ye mete, it shall be measured to you again," is a truth especially manifest in the known approach of death, and in death itself, when all that is responsive to departing excellence speaks out.   As intelligence of her culminating illness and critical danger went abroad to her friends, the sympathy and sorrow that poured in through numerous letters from gifted souls, throughout the length and breadth of the land, and from England and Germany and Spain, showed the fidelity of a nature that could evoke such evidence of wide-spread, unslumbering affection. It were worth the longest life to close it as the center of such love, such honor, such grateful emotion as came to her during her last days and has come to me since her death, from such a number of great and pure souls in spontaneous and tender attestation of her worth. It was a demonstration of the possible pathos in human character, and of the reward and renown which wait on intellect swayed by goodness. The fidelity in her which inspired it was life-long, was so identified with her, was so inflexible, that, with those who knew her intimately, to name her was to say "faithfulness to the right, to the conviction of duty, and to the instincts of changeless affection."

The transcendently endearing quality of her disposition, which was in her character what Raphael's ineffable expression of face is in his Madonnas, was its sweetness. Without any of the monotony of mere amiability, without warping her clear and upright judgment, ever attendant upon the buoyant spirit and brilliancy of her mind, was the warmth and glow of a nature necessarily, "without shadow of turning," truly, deeply kind, that nestled in and clung to all that was benign in life. This it was that made her so gentle to the aged and to the sorrowing; so fond of home; so tenacious of the memories of childhood; so appreciative of truth and refinement; that gave her such quick discernment of uprightness and independence and of culture, such admiration for friendship, such communion with nature, and such reverence for the dead. As the rose, by the law of its development, must, along with its brightness of colors, produce its exhalation of odor, so it was a law of her spiritual being that, along with all her bright thoughts, should come a whispered suggestion of what is gentle and benign and gracious and morally beautiful in existence.

There is imperfection, in any transfer to canvas, of beauty of feature and expression in the natural countenance, and the inability increases with the rise in the degree or order of the beauty sought to be reproduced. How much more of difficulty in the embodiment in adequate description of the peculiarities and inspiring purposes of noble character! How much of the loftiness of her resolves, of her unselfish devotion to the pure and the good, eludes the power of expression, "in matter-molded forms of speech," and how much of the reverence which we felt in witnessing her life remains wanting, as we contemplate its delineation, though affection continually prompted the memory and lingers in every constituent word!

How truly has Lord Bacon said, "That is the best part of beauty which a picture does not (fully) give."

> "What practice, howsoe'er expert,
>   In fitting aptest words to things,   .
>   Or voice, the richest-toned that sings,
>   Hath power to give thee as thou wert!"

IX

Her Last Sickness.

ON the 6th day of February, 1885, in New Orleans, the clouds began to gather in our clear and soft sky never to be dispersed. Then suddenly commenced an illness that baffled all medical skill aided by all the ministrations of affection. For I can now see that from that day she constantly, gradually, declined in strength. When relief was not afforded, her physician from New Haven was summoned, whose presence had ever been to us both, not only that of one highly skilled in his art, but also that of a beloved brother. With his coöperation, the surgeon in attendance was enabled to overcome the immediate cause of danger. Her dear friend, who had been her teacher, gladly came also. The sweet sufferer, as well as I myself, hoped and believed she was progressing toward recovery.

On the 25th of April, I accompanied her and this friend to Washington, where I left them for an anticipated sojourn of three or four weeks, and a subsequent progress to the old home in New Haven, there to await my coming. I returned to my duties in New Orleans. But on the twelfth day of my separation from her, there came evidence that alarmed me; it was an unfinished letter from her to me. So delicately thoughtful and so resolutely active had she ever been to forestall and allay apprehension about her, on my part, that full well I knew her illness must be indeed prostrating. Through the great kindness of Justice Woods, who was then at my house in New Orleans, and of Judge Pardee, a brother judge was assigned to sit in my place, and I immediately hurried on to rejoin her in Washington. Dr. Huntington, of the U. S. Army, a prized friend of college days, in whose medical care I had there left her, accompanied us to New Haven. We were all buoyant with the hope that her reinstatement in the atmosphere and amid the surroundings that had always proved so genial and restorative, and under the medical skill that had so often brought relief, would reëstablish health.

Except for the intrusion of an occasional anxious thought, which we banished as unfounded, the days from May to August were the most supremely

10

happy of all our many blissful days. With the
exception of the servants, we were for the most
part alone. The weather was unusually temperate.
We passed from morning till night in reading
aloud together the sacred and classic writers, and
in the nameless diversions of comfortable illness,
in a home which, through her ingenuity and taste,
was supplied with all that could be desired by the
fastidious in health or by the delicate in sickness.

She filled our joint life with the light of her
cheerfulness. She gave playful names to the
medicines and the wraps for the sick-room which
moved us to laughter, as day after day we repeated
them. Feeble as she was, she was unwearied in
her inventive sportiveness. She strove in every
way to beguile me from anxiety and to dispossess
me of fear. How little did I dream throughout these
halcyon days that so near us "sat that shadow
feared of man,"

" Who broke our fair companionship,
   Who bore thee where I could not see,
   Nor follow, though I walk in haste,
   And think that somewhere in the waste
   That shadow sits and waits for me."

In August, both her physician and we ourselves were convinced that relief could come from
surgery alone. She then determined to avail herself of surgical skill of the highest order and
where its efficacy could be most certainly counted
upon. From this point of time she manifested a
placidity, a calmness, always unruffled. This
outward aspect was the result, in part, of her un-
willingness to add to my distress, which seemed
to weigh more with her than the danger threat-
ening her life; partly of the serious wisdom with
which she met all life's experiences; largely of in-
born vigor of courage, that did but assert and
re-assert itself and increase and rise in its might,
as came, like the billows of a dark sea, the terrible
demands upon it; and most of all, of that high
and holy habit of communion with her Heavenly
Father, which eliminated all terror from events
since they proceeded from Him.

I had learned how tender she was of the feelings of loved ones, how much "she could suppress
of fainting nature's feebleness," how she could
hide all traces of suffering with a smile, even when
she was racked with internal torture. I had seen

too, and that often, how her nature with its fawn-like timidity in the midst of the ways of safety, when critical dangers confronted, took on calmness and courage; but I was unprepared for the disclosures of the very wisdom of composure and the almost hardihood of bravery which she manifested from this time down to the hour of her death. When the two ordeals of suffering through surgery came, after saying the prayer of Stephen this gentle being took leave of me to face her pain and danger with a tranquillity of look and voice and manner, and of her whole being, as absolutely undisturbed as though she had been about to enter a friend's parlor or a place of amusement. She was sustained by more than native courage, fathomless as that quality seemed to be in her bosom; she was also upborne and rendered so delightfully composed by the Christian's faith.

In September, we went to New York by the easiest possible contrivances. Without a murmur or an uttered regret, she left her home, so redolent of tender associations. With a spirit which had the elasticity of the air itself she went through all her succeeding trials,— so manifold and exhausting,— which to one constituted with her exquisite delicacy and sensitiveness must have brought such keen pangs.

For six weeks we were like little children in our joy, buoyant in the belief that a cure had been attained. The seventh week shook our confidence. Misgivings were more frequent, and were harder to be cast out. So steadfastly does absorbing affection cling to what constitutes all that is dear and precious in existence, and refuse to perceive inevitable danger slowly creeping on towards it, that it was not until the last fortnight of her life, that she and I realized that our two beings, which, like the fibers of the wood and bark in the living tree, had closed and adhered and coalesced,— had grown into one,— were to be cleft in twain, to be rent asunder; that the path of one of us was to be "in fields we knew," and of one " in undiscovered lands." O tender human hearts all over the world ! How would you add to your mutually bestowed love, even where it is given in most generous largess; how would you quicken and multiply its swiftest and most numerous ministrations and soften its gentlest utterances; how would you transfer kindness from the sphere of thought and intention to that of life and act, if, beforehand, ye could but half know the broken-heartedness, the suddenness and bitterness of the woe of impending and accomplished separation, which is by survivors called Death ! If ye could even dimly foresee how, though God and duty and hope of Heaven graciously abide, upon the severance of lives truly companioned, to the soul left on the earth there come no more the thrill and ecstasy of newly unfolding being, but rather, amid the veiled and processional events of each to-day, there lingers and stirs the commemoration of a receptive and responsive yesterday, and in spite of prayer and faith existence comes to be an almost unbroken sacrament!

Throughout her illness, growing broader, deeper, vastly enriched towards the close, was the development of her character as a Christian. All through our married life she abhorred cant, and sensitively shrank from often speaking fully, even to me, of her religious experiences. While her religious feelings were intense, she seemed to view them as too sacred to be exhibited to others in set phrases. But they were disclosed with no less certainty and earnestness, and with more striking influence upon others, because uttered only by well-understood reference, or most frequently expressed in some act which showed triumph over, or abnegation of, personal comfort or preference. To her mind Religion was life — not so much a conception as an embodiment; was to be apprehended and taught and striven for, not in any formula of words, nor indeed in single acts, but in the acquisition and observance of habits which were founded on trust in God, a dwelling with Christ, consideration of others and forgetfulness of self; of faith, of sacrifices for faith, of punctuality, neatness, industry, fidelity, truth, kindness, charity, and in painstaking in practicing every virtue that went to make up holy living; to her mind it was something which, viewed as an attainment or an example, was to be not *spoken or read, but lived.* Those who knew her best have rarely known, in life or biography, a human character whose every affiliation was so with what was holy; whose every withdrawal was so from what was sullied, or which could more worthily or signally have share in the beatitude, "Blessed are the pure in heart, for they shall see God." "O ye lilies and other white harbingers of spring, the grace of the fashion whereof is so often and so exquisitely culled by art to be symbols of unspotted purity, what can ye show of silent flowering in the white freedom from all that assoils, which noble woman cannot much better show herself?"

Ever had she loved prayer. It was always our habit, after we had retired to our chamber, to close the day with the Lord's Prayer, the little "Now we lay us down to sleep," which the dear lips of our mothers had respectively taught us, followed by an oral, spontaneous prayer, which was a little mirror wherein was reflected and held up to Him who seeth in secret the image of our souls' inmost, highest daily needs and yearnings. After the commencement of her sickness in February, she seemed to delight more and more in our joint evening outpourings. She seemed to look backwards and forwards to them with a satisfaction which showed they had for her sustaining power. During the early summer, while speaking to that loved friend, to whom she wrote the longing letter about New Haven, of the blessings which during her illness had been vouchsafed to her, she remarked, "*and now Faith has come.*" In New Orleans, in New Haven, and in New-York, she was eager to hear the Scriptures read. With especial fondness did she love to linger on those portions which gave the words of Jesus—most of all His sayings as rendered in the mellifluous accents of St. John. All summer, after the Bible, the book which was her favorite was Canon Farrar's "Life of Christ."

During a portion of her last two weeks on earth there was with us that friend, bound to her by the double tie of early instruction and long and unreservedly enjoyed intimacy, whose prayerful ministrations were so touchingly appreciated by the then consciously dying, uncomplaining sufferer. That friend thus relates what she said:

"'I have learned to meet each day with its burden of suffering, as it comes, one day at a time, trusting in the Lord.' In a time of critical decision a friend repeated the passage, 'Commit thy way unto the Lord—and He ,shall bring it to

11

pass.' Quick as thought, she said: 'You have omitted the *best part*, "trust also in Him,"' and then repeated the whole correctly."

The same friend adds :

"The special requests to be made in the brief prayers of the sick-room evinced a faith that was childlike and inspiring. What she *needed* most was to be asked for as tho' it would be given." One instance of this kind will live in the hearts of survivors : after a weary, sleepless night, followed by a morning of utter restlessness, she called for a prayer: "Pray for sleep *now*." Her voiced "Amen" was followed quickly by folded hands, closed eyes, and peaceful slumber. At intervals, the eyes opened, and those who saw her will not soon forget the grateful, peaceful smile, followed again and again by quiet sleep. The next day she had "something to say" when alone with her friend, who shared her secret ; it was her wish to testify thus :

"Never, in all my life, have I known so wonderful an answer to prayer; the sleep came so quickly," she said with emphasis, "it made God seem near, not far."

Several days before her death, she seemed to physicians, to friends, and to herself to be dying. With serenely composed fidelity of affection and with unfaltering trust, she took leave of friends and of him who was in death, as he had been in life, her other self.

With pious gratitude, with resignation so sweetly and purely unselfish that it was a literal renunciation of self, she culled, as from a garden, from our happy life, a bouquet of blissful memories, and handed it to me with the glory of that which is to be in her voice and look and manner. Then, with the supreme and shining care with which she had crowned my life, lovingly and with the exultation of saints when close to Heaven, she commended to me, as "the one thing in life, preparation to meet God." When (my one great hope of her recovery — so hard to be lost — all gone) my agony could be neither repressed nor hidden, she said to me very gently, but with the pathos and faith of one who saw the realities of Heaven, not the vanishing scenes of Earth, and with a thorough subordination of supremest human love to a love for the Saviour ever transcendent:

"My darling, my Saviour calls me, you must let me go to Him."

From this time to that of the deep sleep which by eight hours preceded death, she seemed filled throughout her whole being — permeated — with a peace which was the overshadowing power of the Spirit world, which illumined her countenance, gave it a radiance like that of the face of Moses when he descended from the mount after a direct and visible communion with God.

It was a transfiguration—a borrowing from a swiftly coming beatification—the rays of a dawning day, "whose waking was to be supremely blest." Her face, like that of the first martyr, "was as it had been the face of an angel." Like him, too, she said: "Lord Jesus, into Thy hands I commit my spirit." She had been permitted to look across the dark waters, into which she was entering, upon the glories of Heaven with a nearness of vision which caused them to be not only revealed by dying words, but also reflected from dying features.

Thus, on January 3d, the first Sabbath of the year, amid the hush which precedes the dawn, with expiring breath, even "from the twilight of eternal day," still whispering — half from Earth, half from Heaven — to a low-bent, unweariedly and fondly attentive ear a final attestation of her love, went forth she, the delicately fashioned, sensitively shrinking one, with the boldness of the long-tried warrior, and the trust of the martyr, into the mystery of death and to the circle of waiting, glorified ones.

It was not merely that this beloved one was in all this

> " So calm and meek,
> So softly worn, so sweetly weak,
> So tearless, yet so tender — kind."

It was not merely that with the shortness of breath came those gleaming flashes of thought and those deep, quickly uttered impassioned words of affection, like the rich staccato notes in music, that will be remembered so fondly in connection with her death.

But her patient endurance of protracted illness and excruciating pains—the fortitude, the heroism with which she underwent danger—her suffering

the pangs of many martyrdoms with naught but
smiles—the sweetness with which she forgot herself in remembering, even in her agony, those she
loved—the composure and resignation at the con-
scious approach of death—her faith in her
Saviour and her undimmed hope of immortality;
these sublime manifestations touched and melted
even the hearts of strangers, and made the naked
walls of the room in the Sanitarium where she
died to glow with an effulgent light that would
have rendered the colors of all Earth's artists pale
and ineffective. Sorrowing, desolated hearts, in the
midst of their anguish, felt the throb of admiration
up to that time unknown, that human nature could
be so grandly and richly endowed, and in its final extremity, by its absorbing and trustful devotion to
what is holy, could so subdue and command. Her
life, from beginning to end, was one piece of rav-
ishing music, ever varying, ever delighting, rich
in its contrasts, sweet in its harmonies, interpreted
and enjoyed most by those most pure, most unselfish, most loving, but melting, swaying, enthralling
all whose ears caught its deep and high diapasons,
gathering fullness of note as character became

grander, and, as she grew into the full proportions of her magnificent womanhood, swelling out into loftier strains made up of more ample chords, and, toward the close, mellowing and becoming more and more sweet, finally falling in softest, receding cadences beyond Earth's silence among Heaven's choral symphonies.

Our loved one's funeral was from that dear old house in Temple street, which was the home of her childhood and the shrine of her maturer years. The Rev. Burdett Hart spoke touchingly in fitting words of faithful narrative, which could not but be those of high and tender eulogy. There was the reading of the sweetest of Mrs. Browning's soul's outpourings, her rendering of the Psalmist's " He giveth His beloved sleep," which had been so often read to and by her, and which was so dear to her. The hymn, "Asleep in Jesus," so precious to her, was sung to a tune associated by us with youthful days, preparatory for life—a tune composed for the sweetest of Moore's rhythmical compositions. Prayer was offered by President Porter, who had united us in marriage. Then forth from the house where had been so zealously and piously gathered and preserved the memorials of childhood and of dear ones, living and departed, and which was so filled with the traces of her taste and culture, we bore that loved form beneath the Gothic arches, bereft of their verdure, and gently laid it in the tomb where slumbers the dust of her kindred, loved by her with such devotion; and, with a weight of sorrow that made our limbs totter like those of infancy and extreme old age, we turned to strive to face the duties of life, from which had gone the presence whose brightness and sweetness and inspiration will be missed and longed for with the pang of unsatisfied hunger and thirst, till we, ourselves, go down to the slumber of silence and to the awakening and to the reunion beyond.

And so, O Holy One, kneeling beside a hearth whose fire Thou hast put out, we lift weary hands to Thee and we pray: Thou who, though Thou wast the Resurrection and the Life, and though Thine eyes had gazed upon the fullness of immortality before the world was, nevertheless didst from those eyes shed tears at the grave of mortal friend, and thereby didst forever honor and hal-

low grief for the loved and loving dead; be Thou
pitiful to us, whose grief, though it fills the height
and length and breadth and depth of our whole
being, is not greater than the measure of the love-
liness of our dead. We hear Thy voice yet being
borne down the ages, from that upper chamber,
in accents still tremulous with tender solicitude
for Thy loved ones, about to be desolated by
Thine own death, saying: "I will not leave you
comfortless," and "I pray for those also, who, in
all coming time, shall believe on My name."
Redeem this Thy promise to us as we quiver and
writhe under the chariot wheels of Thy chastening
Providence, and strive, through thick and fast falling tears, to see not wrath, but love.

Enable us to say, not as ending a vain struggle,
but with the sweet spirit of obedient children,
"Thy will be done." Thou who hast taught us
the capacity of the soul for suffering, by taking
her who was the grace and joy of life, fill the extended void with the power of the Saviour's Presence and with the peace given by Him. We
thank Thee for the measureless blessings of the
companionship and love of one possessing such an

12

assemblage of exalted qualities and for the sacred hope of reunion with her; may our grief not expend itself in selfish repinings, but rather find expression in the imitation, to the extent of our ability, of her shining virtues. May the influence from her unfaltering allegiance to the right, blended with that of her tenderest love for us, continually beat in our lives like pulses in our veins and move us on to noble ends. Grant us faith and strength wherewith to perform all life's duties with courage unabated by reason of great sorrow. May we ever heed her final admonition. May we "live disinterestedly, live for immortality," and "whatever of riches, or renown, or joy, or affection we would rescue from final dissolution, may we lay up in God."

O suffering, reigning Christ, Man of Sorrows, God of Love, Saviour of the dead and the living, we pray Thee, by thy Crown of Thorns and Thy Crown of Glory, that through Thy grace we may so walk with Thee on the earth, to such a degree keep pace with our dead in their unfettered progress, and so daily and hourly grow in wisdom and worship and charity, that when we awake in Thy likeness we may not fail of their companionship!

APPENDIX.

Announcement of her death in the New Orleans Picayune,
January 4, 1886.

DEATH OF MRS. E. C. BILLINGS.

THE sad announcement was made yesterday, by telegram, to friends in this city, from Hon. E. C. Billings, Judge of the United States District Court, that Mrs. Billings had died in New York City at half-past two o'clock yesterday morning. Mrs. Billings had been ill for some time, and her demise was not unexpected. This estimable lady was well known and greatly esteemed in this city. Her amiable disposition, bright intelligence, and gentleness of manner endeared her to all with whom she came in contact. The news of her death will be received with real sorrow by the residents of this city, who recognized her admirable qualities, and Judge Billings will have their warm sympathy in his great affliction.

The funeral will take place on Wednesday, in New Haven, Conn., of which city the deceased was a native.

Orders of the United States Courts, sitting in New Orleans, out of respect to her memory.

UNITED STATES CIRCUIT COURT.

[Judge DON A. PARDEE.]

THE court being advised of the death of Mrs. E. C. Billings, wife of the Hon. E. C. Billings, United States District Judge of this district, one of the Judges of this court, it is ordered that the causes set for to-day be continued until to-morrow, and that the court be adjourned in respect to her memory and as an expression of sympathy and condolence with our colleague.

UNITED STATES DISTRICT COURT.

[Judge ALECK BOARMAN, presiding.]

ON opening of the court yesterday, Mr. J. W. Gurley, Assistant United States Attorney, suggested the death of Mrs. E. C. Billings, wife of Hon. Edward C. Billings, Judge of this court, and thereupon moved, as a mark of sympathy in his bereavement, and of respect for her memory, that the court be adjourned.   Mr. William Grant having seconded the motion, on behalf of the bar, in brief and appropriate terms, his Honor, Judge Boarman, expressing his full concurrence in the propriety of the motion, ordered that the court be adjourned.

Obituary Notice published in the New Orleans Times-Democrat, January 31, 1886. Communicated anonymously from Hartford, Conn.

EMILY SANFORD BILLINGS.

[*Communicated.*]

DIED, in New York City, Jan. 3, 1886, Mrs. Emily Sanford Billings, wife of Judge Edward C. Billings, of New Orleans, La., and daughter of the late Hervey Sanford, of New Haven, Conn.

It seems fitting that more than the announcement of the death of this gifted woman should find a place in your columns. For, in New Orleans, where Mrs. Billings spent the winter months, her gentle courtesy and rare intelligence were enjoyed by many appreciative friends.

In her earlier married life, as the wife of Capt. Armstrong, she will be remembered as a favorite among the brilliant men and women of naval circles, at the different navy yards where her husband was stationed.

At New Haven, Mrs. Billings's birthplace, and where she passed her early days, she greatly endeared herself to kindred and friends by the fidelity of her attachments, and the talents and accomplishments which made her the congenial companion of literary men and women. Her loyal heart delighted in the memories and associations which made the old home under the historic elms particularly dear; and to this shrine came many distinguished men and women to enjoy the graceful hospitality and interchange of thought which will never be forgotten.

It did not seem to lookers-on that the great happiness of mutual devotion which characterized Mrs. Billings's married life was soon to be severed. Existence was dear to her affectionate nature, and she knew it was given her as a blessing for others. An ample fortune set no limits to the pleasures of travel, benevolence, or the pursuit of knowledge, and upon two homes are left the impresses of her taste and refinement.

So oft had ever-watchful care averted the dangers which threatened the delicate organization which Mrs. Billings inherited, that friends hoped against hope, when fewer letters from her pen and sad tidings from others told of the limitations imposed by failing strength.

Coming North last summer under a physician's care, she sought to disarm the fears of anxious friends by the bright smile and cheerful greeting with which she met their expressions of solicitude. Those who were privileged to be with the invalid in her long confinement to her room, felt that it was the chamber of peace ; for weakness and many a pang, which none but the sufferer realized, did but ripen the faith which was so soon to be changed to sight. When medical skill failed in its mission of relief, and the vigilance and devotion of loved ones and faithful nurses no longer availed, Mrs. Billings, with characteristic heroism, decided to place herself under the care of a distinguished surgeon, seeking to prolong life through an ordeal from which many a strong man shrinks.

At first it seemed that recovery, so prayerfully sought, was to be granted; but the angel of death had but tarried with his message. Ere the early dawn of the first Sabbath of the new year had touched the horizon, a group of heart-stricken watchers gathered around the death-bed of the beloved wife, sister, friend. But their tender ministrations could no longer detain the soul that heard the voice of God calling to fairer worlds on high. The sensitive spirit feared no evil, safe in the embrace of its Guide and Comforter, and the shadows of death were illuminated by the light of immortality.

In unison with such a departure are the following lines of a Christian poet:

> " When the last summons comes to me,
>   Like angel whispering, let it be:
> ' The Master comes and calls for thee ! '
>   And friends who final vigils keep
>   With this glad thought will cease to weep:
> ' He giveth His beloved sleep.' "

Interesting funeral services at New Haven, at which President Porter, of Yale, and the Rev. Burdett Hart officiated, were followed by burial in the old cemetery in which the Sanford tomb stands.

HARTFORD, CONN., January 23, 1886.   X.

An epitomized characterization of her contained in an extract from a letter, written by Mr. Justice William B. Woods, dated January 20, 1886.

"SINCE I saw the form of your dear wife committed to the keeping of Mother Earth, my mind has dwelt much on her life and character. For intelligence, prudence, and good judgment, she had few equals. Her mind had been trained in the best schools, and she had been cultured by much travel and the best society; she was a most interesting and delightful companion, and a most truly constant and faithful friend. But her great charm to me was the heavenly sweetness of her disposition."

www.ingramcontent.com/pod-product-compliance
Lightning Source LLC
Chambersburg PA
CBHW032157010726
47493CB00008BA/2728